Artists Through the Ages

Mary Cassatt

Alix Wood

WINDMILL BOOKS

New York

Published in 2016 by **Windmill Books**, An Imprint of Rosen Publishing
29 East 21st Street, New York, NY 10010

Editor for Alix Wood Books: Eloise Macgregor
Designer: Alix Wood

Photo Credits: Cover, 1, 15 © Metropolitan Museum of Art; 4, 13 © Smithsonian Institute; 5 © The British Library; 6 © Art Renewal Center; 8 © Life Magazine; 9 left © Louvre Museum; 11, 28-29 © Christie's Images/Artothek; 16-17, 21 © nga/Collection of Mr. and Mrs. Paul Mellon; 19 © Art Institute of Chicago; 22 © Mr. and Mrs. James Barker; 23, 24 © nga/ Chester Dale Collection; 25 © Terra Foundation for American Art; 27 © Woodmere Art Museum, Philadelphia; all other images are in the public domain

Cataloging-in-Publication Data
Wood, Alix.
Mary Cassatt / by Alix Wood.
p. cm. — (Artists through the ages)
Includes index.
ISBN 978-1-4777-5597-6 (pbk.)
ISBN 978-1-4777-5596-9 (6 pack)
ISBN 978-1-4777-5452-8 (library binding)
1. Cassatt, Mary, — 1844-1926 — Juvenile literature.
2. Artists — United States — Biography — Juvenile literature.
I. Wood, Alix. II. Title.
N6537.C35 W66 2016
759.13—d23

Manufactured in the United States of America
CPSIA Compliance Information: Batch #WS15WM:
For Further Information contact Windmill Books, New York, New York at 1-866-478-0556

Contents

Who Was Cassatt?

Mary Cassatt was born near Pittsburgh, Pennsylvania in 1844. She was one of seven children, but two died very young. Her family was wealthy. Her father, Robert, was a **stockbroker** and **land agent**. Her mother, Katherine, was from a banking family and was well-educated.

Mary Cassatt, around age 70

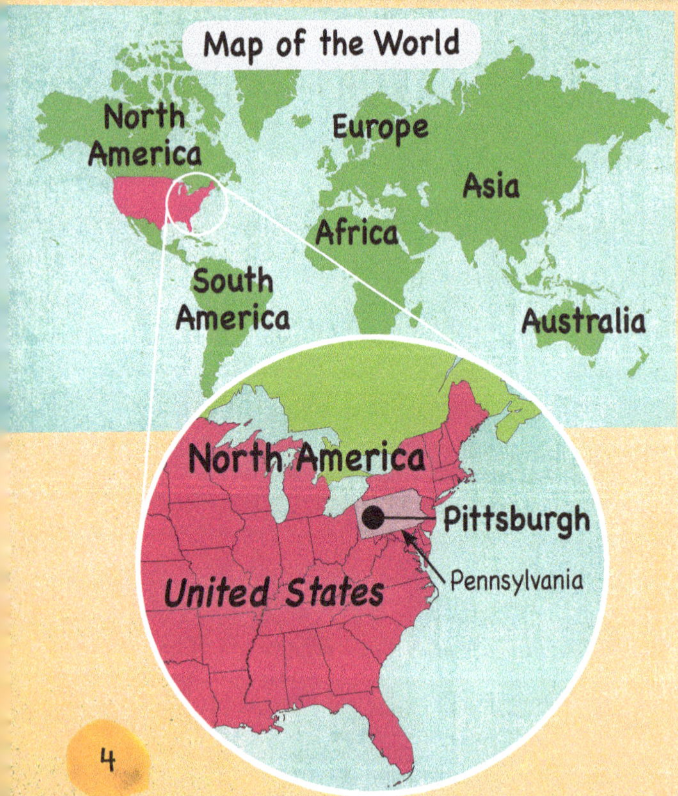

Cassatt's family thought travel was an important part of their children's education. As a child Mary spent five years in Europe. Her family visited many of Europe's capital cities. She could speak both French and German.

Cassatt went to the Pennsylvania Academy of the Fine Arts at age 16. Cassatt's family did not want her to become a professional artist. Most women students at that time did not take up art as a job. However, Cassatt was different!

Leaving the Academy

Cassatt became frustrated at the slow pace of teaching at the Academy. Although around 20 percent of the students were women, the teachers refused to allow female students to draw from **life models**. Cassatt decided to leave the Academy after four years.

Pennsylvania Academy of the Fine Arts

Women and Careers

Cassatt moved to Paris in 1866 to study art. Her father objected, but her mother went with her to be sure she was safe. In the 1860s it was unusual for wealthy women to want a career. Women usually learned to care for the home and perhaps sew or paint as a hobby.

Women were not allowed to go to the famous Paris art school, the École des Beaux-Arts. Cassatt studied privately with masters who also taught at the school. She studied under well-known artists such as Jean-Léon Gérôme and Thomas Couture. She also learned by copying the great paintings hanging at the Louvre museum.

Jean-Léon Gérôme

In 1868, one of Cassatt's paintings, *A Mandoline Player*, was accepted to be **exhibited** by the famous Paris Salon. Cassatt and her American artist friend Elizabeth Jane Gardner became the first American women to exhibit there. She painted *A Mandoline Player* in a Romantic style similar to Thomas Couture's, one of her teachers.

An Alias

Cassatt's father did not support her career as an artist. He once said that he would almost rather see her dead! Perhaps this is why she signed *A Mandoline Player* "Mary Stevenson." Stevenson may have been her middle name.

A Mandoline Player, 1868

Bad Luck in the U.S.

In 1870, a war broke out between France and Prussia. Cassatt returned to the United States to her parents' new house near Philadelphia. She found it hard to paint there. Her father wanted to discourage her from being an artist and refused to pay for any art supplies.

To raise some money for art equipment, Cassatt tried selling her paintings in New York, but no one bought them. She got her paintings exhibited in Chicago, but tragically lost them all in the Great Chicago Fire of 1871.

An illustration showing the ruins of Chicago after the fire in 1871

Luckily, Cassatt was asked by the archbishop of Pittsburgh to copy two famous religious paintings by Correggio that were hanging in Parma, Italy. Cassatt could return to Europe and be paid for her work! With the money she earned she managed to stay in Europe and keep on painting.

Learning Her Craft

During her months copying Correggio in Parma, Cassatt studied his and other Italian masters' paintings. Her painting below right shows how her style was influenced by them.

A painting by Correggio

Two Women Throwing Flowers During Carnival, painted by Cassatt in 1872

Painting Mothers

Cassatt is perhaps best known for painting women, particularly mothers with their children. The bond with her own mother was strong. Cassatt's mother Katherine was a great supporter of her daughter. She traveled with her during her early trips to Europe. She was also the model for some of Cassatt's best portraits.

Cassatt painted her mother in 1878, reading the French newspaper *Le Figaro*. The painting was praised by **critics** at an exhibition in New York, who said it was the best painting there. Being able to read a French newspaper shows how well her mother had settled into French life.

A Proud Father

Even Cassatt's father was pleased with this portrait of his wife. He sent *Reading Le Figaro* to Mary's brother Alexander in Philadelphia with a note saying "I hope you will be pleased with the portrait, in fact I do not allow myself doubt that you will be."

Reading Le Figaro.
A portrait of Mary Cassatt's mother painted in 1878.

Traveling Influences

After finishing her paintings for the archbishop, Cassatt decided to travel. She went to Madrid and Seville in Spain. Great Spanish painters and the Spanish way of life influenced her work.

Cassatt was inspired by the art she had seen in Spain. She worked on a group of paintings with a Spanish influence, including *Spanish Dancer Wearing a Lace Mantilla*. The painting was shown at the Paris Salon in 1874.

An Admirer

Cassatt's painting was admired by the French painter Edgar Degas. Degas was said to have remarked "It is true. There is someone who feels as I do." Perhaps he felt her style and the subject matter were similar to his own paintings of ballet dancers.

Spanish Dancer Wearing a Lace Mantilla, 1873

Settling in Paris

After touring Belgium, Holland, and Italy, Cassatt settled back in Paris, France, in 1874. She set up a **studio** and started to work. Soon, her parents and elder sister Lydia joined her.

Cassatt was close to her sister. They shared an apartment in Paris. Lydia would often model for Cassatt. There are eleven known paintings of Lydia. She modeled for Cassatt's work, *The Cup of Tea*. If you look closely at the painting you can see the texture of the **canvas** showing through. Art critics thought this was sloppy and criticized the painting. Modern critics think it adds life to the painting.

A Loss

Lydia died in 1882 of kidney disease. Her death upset Cassatt so much that she didn't paint for some time afterward.

The Cup of Tea, painted around 1880

Edgar Degas

Edgar Degas was a member of a group of **Impressionist** artists in Paris at that time. Impressionist artists got their name because they painted an impression of a scene, as if they had just taken a glimpse of it, rather than studied it for hours. The paintings are usually very lively and bright.

Mary Cassatt used to go to a Paris art dealer's store and stare at the work by Degas. She said his paintings changed her life. One day Degas came to her studio and asked her to join his group of artists. The group included famous artists Claude Monet, Auguste Renoir, and Camille Pissarro. Cassatt was very happy.

Degas encouraged her in her work. Cassatt developed her use of color and light. She exhibited paintings at the group's exhibitions, such as *Little Girl in a Blue Armchair*, below.

Little Girl in a Blue Armchair, 1878

The Child's Bath

Most Impressionists painted **landscapes** and street scenes. Cassatt became well-known for **portraits**. She liked to paint women in everyday situations. She especially liked to paint mothers with their children.

The Child's Bath shows a mother washing her child. The bold patterns and outlines of the painting are very similar to Japanese art. The colorful patterns of the dress and carpet **contrast** against the pale child. This helps draw your eye to the child in the painting first.

You're Not My Mother!

Almost all of the models for Cassatt's mother and child portraits were not actually related at all! She preferred to choose her models individually so they fit the situation she wanted to paint.

The Child's Bath, 1898

Painting Children

When Cassatt painted children she painted them as they really were. She did not make the children look overly cute, as many artists at the time did. Cassatt captured their awkward movements and odd expressions with great skill.

In her painting *Children Playing on the Beach*, Cassatt paints the children's clumsy movements beautifully. The little girl in front is clutching her shovel oddly in her fist. With her legs sprawled to help her balance, she concentrates on filling her bucket with sand.

Children Playing on the Beach, 1884

Child in a Straw Hat, painted around 1886

Japanese Influences

In 1890, Cassatt went to an exhibition of Japanese prints in Paris. It inspired her to experiment with printmaking. She saw prints like this one by Kitagawa Utamaro. She started using the simple modern shapes in her own work.

A print by Kitagawa Utamaro that may have inspired Cassatt

See the Similarities

The positions of the figures in Cassatt's *The Fitting*, right, are similar to Utamaro's work. The patterns and areas of **flat color** were similar, too. Also Utamaro recorded the everyday life of women, just as Cassatt did.

The Fitting is part of a series of ten prints that Cassatt created between 1890-91.

The Boating Party

One of Cassatt's best known works is *The Boating Party*. It was the centerpiece of her exhibition in 1895. She used flat areas of bright color and strong shapes. Do you find your eye looks at the baby first? Cassatt cleverly uses the shapes of the adults' arms, the sail, and the oar to point to the baby.

The Boating Party painted around 1894

Summertime

In the same year, 1894, Cassatt painted a more relaxed boating scene, *Summertime*. A woman and child watch ducks from a boat on a lake. The brushstrokes are much more visible in this painting.

The Later Years

In 1894, Cassatt moved out of Paris and to a large house in the French countryside. She lived there happily and painted. In 1910, she went on a trip to Egypt with her brother, Gardner. The trip had a big efffect on Cassatt.

The beautiful artwork that she saw on her trip made her question her own ability to paint. Also, while in Egypt her brother became ill, and died shortly after they returned. These two events shook Cassatt and she was unable to paint for some time.

Losing Sight

Cassatt suffered from ill health and failing eyesight in later life. Because of her poor eyesight she could not see to paint. Instead she created prints from some of her earlier work. By the time of her death she was completely blind.

The Pink Sash, a pastel drawing from around 1898

Legacy

Cassatt died in 1926 at age 82. She helped change people's beliefs about art and women artists. Her paintings are in many museum collections around the world.

One of Cassatt's most important **legacies** was that she encouraged wealthy Americans to buy Impressionist art. She asked the collectors to promise to eventually pass on the paintings to American art museums for others to see and study. This helped generations of young American artists. It is thanks to her efforts that many Impressionist paintings are in American art collections today.

A Goodnight Hug, 1880

Tender Images

Cassatt's paintings celebrating the bond between mothers and their children is her lasting legacy.

Glossary

canvas (KAN-ves)
A piece of cloth used as a surface for painting.

contrast (KON-trast)
Noticeable differences between things, particularly color or brightness.

critics (KRIH-tikz)
People who make or give a judgment of the value, worth, beauty, or excellence of something.

exhibited (ek-ZIH-bit-ed)
Shown in public for people to see.

flat color
(FLAT KUH-ler)
Areas of color with a smooth unchanging surface.

Impressionist
(im-PREH-shuh-nist)
An artist who concentrates on the impression of a scene using unmixed primary colors and small brushstrokes to simulate light.

land agent
(LAND AY-jent)
A realtor who specializes in land sales.

landscapes (LAND-skaypz) Pictures of the natural scenery.

legacies (LEH-guh-seez) Things that have been handed down from another person.

life models (LYF MAH-dulz) Models who pose for artists to draw.

portraits (POR-tretz) Pictures, often paintings, of a person.

stockbroker (STOK BROH-kur) A person who buys and sell stocks.

studio (STOO-dee-oh) The working place of an artist.

Websites

For web resources related to the subject of this book, go to: **www.windmillbooks.com/weblinks** and select this book's title.

Read More

Harris, Lois. *Mary Cassatt: Impressionist Painter*. New Orleans: LA Pelican Publishing, 2007.

O'Connor, Jane. *Mary Cassatt: Family Pictures* (Smart About Art). New York, NY: Grosset & Dunlap, 2003.

Zaczek, Iain. *Mary Cassatt* (Great Artists). New York, NY: Gareth Stevens, 2014.

Index